Caroline De Filippi

Venetia Victrix and other Poems

Caroline De Filippi

Venetia Victrix and other Poems

ISBN/EAN: 9783337398149

Printed in Europe, USA, Canada, Australia, Japan

Cover: Foto ©Andreas Hilbeck / pixelio.de

More available books at **www.hansebooks.com**

VENETIA VICTRIX

AND OTHER POEMS

BY

CAROLINE FITZ GERALD

London

MACMILLAN AND CO.

AND NEW YORK

1889

CONTENTS

VATES IGNOTUS

YE gods that, from Olympus' height,

    Lean to the music of his lyre,

Who binds the world in links of light,

    Consenting to the high desire

    That turns pure hearts to meet his fire,

What time long shadows leave the grass,

And heaven's clear echoes cloudward pass

    To swell his earth's responsive choir;

B

Wise shapers of our human ways,

    Immortal ones by Fate's decree,

    Holding the chain of our brief days

      As holds a maiden, in her glee,

      A chain of blossoms by the sea,

    To shed them singly in the wave—

      Ye gods, the days are dear to me

Ye drop so deftly in the grave.

Therefore I turn to thee whose hand

      First struck the magic chords whence sprang

      The wondrous lays wise Orpheus sang,

Compelling quiet through the land,

Till lo ! the forest creatures stand

      Entrancéd by those strains of yore,

      From reedy fen or fallow hoar,

Fearless and fain—a silent band !

I see the years before me roll,

    Turning my life to lifeless clay;

I see each far-off prophet-soul

    Touched by the fingers of thy day;

    Down the dim aisles I hear men say:

" A singer of the Grecian land,

    An unknown name, a nameless hand—

    One moulder of the giant lay!"

Apollo, lo! thy lay is mine!

    Some strain I hear, some note I grasp,

    Some harmony enfold, and clasp

Some beam from that bright brow of thine!

Grant swifter words, O power divine,

    A fuller voice to sing to thee,

    A subtler sense to hear and see

The song and splendour of thy shrine!

VENETIA VICTRIX

In Paris, at the window, MONSIEUR LE DOCTEUR D——
Chevalier de la Légion d'Honneur, etc. (Anno 184-?)

How far-off Venice seems to-night !   How dim
The still-remembered sunsets, with the rim
Of gold round the stone haloes, where they stand,
Those carven saints, and look towards the land,
Right Westward, perched on high, with palm in hand,

Completing the peaked church-front.   Oh how clear

And dark against the evening splendour !   Steer

Between the graveyard island and the quay,

Where North-winds dash the spray on Venice ;—see

The rosy light behind dark dome and tower,

Or gaunt smoke-laden chimney ;—mark the power

Of Nature's gentleness, in rise or fall

Of interlinkéd beauty, to recall

Earth's majesty in desecration's place,

Lending yon grimy pile that dream-like face

Of evening beauty ;—note yon ragged cloud,

Red-rimmed and heavy, drooping like a shroud

Over Murano in the dying day.

I see it now as then—so far away !

In Paris, here, the sleet drives on the pane,

Harder and yet more hard, from noonday's rain

Freezing in sheet-ice.   On the thin-glazed street

Slip horses—men too, women—see, bare feet,

Bent shoulders, yon pale wistful boy, who stands

Clutching his basket in thin shivering hands !

I thought I marked some likeness in that face.—

Perhaps a friend of years gone by ?   I'll trace

The thought back.   Will he turn the corner there ?

No, down again !—Ah, we may sit and stare !

Warm window-seat, red firelight through the room,

Just waiting for a lamp to clear the gloom,

And light your story's leaf,—and all the while—

But where did I once see that same strange smile,

Defiant, as of joy contained in self ?

Now look ! the basket saved, what ails the elf ?

What ! Up the steps ? Surely not bound for church !

Hear the wind howl !—Now see—another lurch !

Not down this time, though ! through the portal, in

At last, like souls in harbour safe from sin.

The dark door swings behind him.   All our street

Left silent, save wild wind and drifting sleet.

Now lamplight—play for you and work for me.

Only that warm smile troubled me.   I see

A ward in Venice—Oh, you look surprise?

True, you saw Venice with such different eyes,

Mere tourist, guide in hand.

                   Long years ago,

New turned forth on the world (as men, you know,

Are turned out finished from the training mill,

Examination-wise, meet to fulfil

Labour allotted in the hungry world,

Just in their narrow sphere), wings new unfurled

In unsubstantial liberty, my right

To practise healing-arts as valid quite

As any man's in Paris—lack of this

One little thing seemed doomed to turn amiss

Ambition vaulting—as you see to-day,

Red-ribbon and the rest !   Trifles you'll say

To talent, perseverance—one slight thing,

Yet key to much, we call an opening.

It came at last, in most unlooked-for way.

My Mother was from Venice. Now one day

There called a strange physician, grave and gray,

Who said he knew my Mother, years ago,

Living among her kin in Venice,—so

He sought her son for old acquaintance' sake.

He liked me, grew my friend. In brief, to make

A long tale short, he offered me a post

In Venice' hospital. 'Twere scarce a boast

To hint he judged me wisely. Deep and sure

That lifelong study of man's heart,—and pure

From all ambition. Such unworldliness

I have not met, joined with such power to bless

The world, whose crowns it never stooped to crave.

All my false pride fell at that touch.—Just brave

I stood and young and earnest. Venice then

Became my home for years, and much of men

I learned; but this one thing, most strange of all,

I felt yon haggard boy's faint smile recall,

So brave and hopeless.

     'Twas an April day,

The year Napoleon's troops took Venice—say

The twenty-fifth of April. All alone

Walking the ward, I heard a sick man moan,

In tones so piteous, as his heart would break :

"Lost, lost, and lost again—for Venice' sake !"

I turned. There lay a man no longer young,

Wasted with fever. I had marked, none hung

About his bed, as friends, with tenderness,

And, when the priest went by, he spared to bless,

Glancing perplexed—perhaps mere sullenness.

I stooped and questioned : "What is lost, my friend?"

"My soul is lost, and now draws near the end.

My soul is surely lost. Send me no priest !

They sing and solemnise the marriage feast

Of man's salvation in the house of love,

And I in Hell, and God in Heaven above,

And Venice safe and fair on earth between,—

No love of mine—mere service—for my Queen."

He paused. I answered him, with such vain words

As practised sight of suffering oft affords,

And muttered as I went : "Great loss forsooth !

Their precious priestcraft ! Now, in Nature's truth,

Why should earth's misery be thus augmented

By moonstruck phantasies sick brains invented

Ages ago? Let thought dwell in thought's tether

Of absolute knowledge. Bring your facts together,

Draw your conclusions, live your life, have done !

This priestcraft ! Half the evils 'neath the sun

Its fostering arts produce—half, would prevent,

Only—mislaid prescription ! Well, repent,

Poor dying sinner ! So you've lost your soul ?

No doubt the gap stands white in God's own scroll.

His soul, he said.—Scarce could one lose much more !

A man's soul is—it means—why, worth a score

(In his own eyes) of lives. What hope and terror,

Ambition, disappointment, pain and error,

All in this life of mine ! while he supposes

His life the curtain-veil, one day discloses

The deathless glory. If I meet their priest,

I'll speak of this. My point of view, at least,

Demands more quiet in the patient's mind.

Much as I shun these topics, still 'twere blind

Wholly to scorn such outer aid as seems

Thrown in our path, and thus the end redeems

The tortuous means." Ah well, I left resolved

To find their "leech of souls"—but straight involved

In work almost beyond my force, new claims

Of care and duty called me from the aims

So lightly formed.

Next week ('twas April's close

Before May brings the promise of her rose,

And, on the mainland plain, green vine and corn

Were budding for the French), since early morn,

From Padua's plain, the dull artillery roar,

Like far-off thunder over the low shore,

Doomed Doge and council, met in trembling state,

To witness Venice' fall—for soon or late

The propless fabric, tottering o'er the sea,

Must sink within the surges silently.

And in the dusk I sat—as now I sit

By the cold pane, and press my brow on it,

Because the old thoughts press—as then the new

Pressed hot and eager, through the holy dew

Of hope, and freedom, and that young redress

Of all earth's ancient wrong they rose to bless

From heart and lips in utter singleness.

And—(being, you see, a stranger)—all the while

I thought of Venice' fall with scarce a smile.

"One empty mummery more whelmed in the past!

Their grief, so seeming-bitter, cannot last

Beyond belief in custom's honoured law.

Some interest may cling, some ancient saw

Invest the past with splendour.   For truth's sake

Let us weed one more lie out!—None will break

The patriot heart or shed the freeman's tear

When Venice' commonwealth lies on the bier."

   Well, as I mused, a knocking on the door,

A summons—sickness—death!   No moment more

Permitted me to muse.   And soon I stood

Beside one bed, in all that solitude

Of concentrated suffering's bated breath,

New marked his own by the hot hand of death—

The same who raved of his lost soul before,

Now sought to see me—not the priest—and o'er

The thin face passed a smile, so brave and good,

Yet somehow hopeless.   Then, in eager mood,

He spoke,—as if he held Death at arm's length

Just to gain time,—with strangely mustered strength :

" I have a tale—so much imports to know

For Venice' sake and mine, before the foe

Shall claim my last surrender.   Kneel and hear,

Lest he, my master, enter !   Never fear,

God having marked you for His own.—God's guest,

Among the golden mansions of the blest,

You will forget.   Remember now awhile !

But waste no prayers on me !"   Once more that smile

Lit the wan face, then waned.   " I am, by trade,

A seaman," he continued, " and unlade

The maple-freight shipped from Dalmatian shore

Beside Giudecca, and the sullen roar

Of wintry storms is ever in mine ear,

And, when the long red sunbeams reach me here,

They kindle the white bed, as once the foam

In my ship's wake, and, in my heart, I roam

Among the Eastern islets.   Oh for space,

Air, freedom !—Hush ! the hour draws on apace.

I sailed, last tenth of April, with one mate,—

Ship *Napoli.*   Now all my heart was hate,

Brimming with hate, pure hate and nought beside.

Mine enemy ! what though his world was wide,

Mine narrow—spoiled all through his scheming.   Then

He took the house—But he was of the ten,

I, a poor sailor.   True the house is gone,

And all are dead.   You see I lived alone,

So thought about the dead.   The quarrel was old,

But when I hear his name my heart turns cold,

Ceases to beat—just hatred !   All the same,

So much shall die with me to praise or blame,

So much imports not.   Only in this fit

Of utter hate, somehow, in my dull wit,

His name grew one with Venice.   For, you see,

He helped to govern Venice.   As for me,

My hatred glanced off from the cool contempt

With which he sat aloft, elate, exempt

From all retaliation—save the knife.

But, grant his death had put an end to strife,

Still stared disaster in my face.   You know,

I was not meet to fight a noble, so

My foster-brother lived.

                Early that day,

The tenth of April, I was gone to pray

For safe return before the shrine we use,

St. Mary's of the Sea.   I could not choose,

Through all my prayer before that holy shrine,

But brood, in anger, on this hate of mine,

Wherefore my prayer was naught.   The blessed morn

Seemed sunlight frozen—like the cold world's scorn.

Then I rose up in wrath, and strode away,

And sat upon the marble well-head.   Day

Was scarce an hour old.   Women came and went

Already, with their copper pails, and leant

And chattered by the well.   One saw my face,

Shuddered and turned, as from a curséd place.

A strange unease fell on the prating group.

Each went her way.   Then did I turn, and stoop,

Where I had spied a little glittering blade,—

Dropped haply by some gallant,—and I played

With the carved death upon the ivory hilt,

And slender snake—smooth image of the guilt

I pondered.—For my course grew sudden plain

And all my hesitation fled.—Such gain

Was mine—crime wished changed to crime dared!—

    anon

I laid the dagger on the smooth-worn stone,

The well-head's rim, and kneeling there, between

Our Lady's shrine, and the grim tool, unseen,

Alone, I swore the oath.   Mark well the words,

Wherein lies half the truth my tale affords—

Now festering in my soul like venomed swords.

I said : 'Because this man has dared to turn

Boy's malice to man's hatred, and discern

His safety in my feebleness, just cause

In scorn for trampling God's and Nature's laws ;—

Because my hatred for him burns my soul ;

Because, through him, I fail to find the goal

Of peace in prayer ; because this hate of mine

Drives me outcast in wrath from Heaven's pure shrine,

As if the deed were done I dare not name ;

Because I reap God's anger, and man's blame,

With mine own thirst for vengeance unallayed ;

Because my heart was mute while my lips prayed ;

Because my mother and mine only love

Lie on lone Lido, where the sands above

Mark not their resting-place ; because earth's crimes

Cry out on Heaven, and these wild woful times

Of war and terror speak of vengeance strange

For greed set up on high, yea, violent change

And comfort for earth's sorrow—hear me, Hell!

Gape wide for me, unless, as I foretell

This hour, and swear, by Mary's holy throne,

The day of my return define mine own

Dim limit of life's passion—this man's death!

Gape wide for me if, till my latest breath,

I ever lift my hand for Venice' good,—

Because he helps her, and his least vile mood

(Which I begrudge) is this same gratitude.'

This said, I rose and wiped the pointed blade,

And laid it sheathed upon my heart, nor stayed

Longer, but sought my mate, and in the bark

Made all things ready.

         Just two hours ere dark

Was flood-tide on the tenth, and we must sail

Eastward across the main, by calm or gale,

To choose among Dalmatian winter's store

Of stout felled trunks, a whole long week before

The earliest craft that season. So we weighed

Our anchor by Giudecca, when the shade

Of evening fell upon the gleaming domes,

And, past the city with its silent homes,

And noisy wharves, we sailed where the broad sea

Laps with its long surf-line round Italy—

Aye, round all earth, folk say. Dim in the gloom

Of gathering dusk lay Venice. When the boom

Of sunset signal died away, I said :

''The coast is cleared, and every red sail spread,

And I am weary. Let me lie and sleep

Here on the deck till midnight clouds the deep ;

Then will I wake and watch for you till day.

There's evil in yon sky. Wake, watch, and pray !'

So then I laid me down—but through my dreams

There crept a haunting terror, still as streams

Deep in the fen-land—like a loveless ghost,

So pallid, craving vengeance from the coast

Of fierce hell-fire, where its weird kind are mewed,

And, starting from my sleep, my brow bedewed

With a nameless dread I could not call to mind,

I heard my comrade, through the piping wind,

Summon me from my rest in drowsy tone,

And grope his way below.   I leaned alone

Over the vessel's side, and watched the sea,

And then a strange old tale came back to me,

Which once would fill my childish soul with dread.

Now all the years between seemed past and dead.

Once more I saw my mother's dark slim form

Lean o'er the water white with wailing storm,

The narrow water by the low house-door,

And watching as for one that came no more,

Croon the same worn old story o'er and o'er:

' *There dwelt a boatman by the waterside*

Who sold his soul to Satan all for pride,

And Satan bought the soul in high disdain,

For in Heaven's loss sees Satan aye Hell's gain ;

So in Charon's wherry seven bold fiends anon

Set sail for Venice o'er the water wan ;

But the wild sea-waves fled from the accursèd bark

And drove the storm on Venice, fierce and dark ;'

Well, so the song runs on.   You know the rest,

How George and Nicholas and Mark the blest

Saved our doomed city from the ship of flame,

So through the night that ancient legend came,

With many a gentler strain of vanished song,

And all the pale array of brows that throng

When Heaven seems very far away—too far

For Desolation's voice.—And now one star

Peered through a lonely cloud-rift, on the rim

Of Eastern ocean—swimming faint and dim

In the heavy air with red fantastic gleams.—

Redder it waxed and greater! As in dreams

I gazed, without the power to move one limb,

And then I lifted up our fisher's hymn

To Mary Maris Stella—my soul shrank

From the pure loud ringing tones, and my voice sank

In a hoarse whisper on the trembling lip.

Then sudden, through the stoutly timbered ship,

I felt the dull jar of a sullen shock!—

Yet peaceful was the flood, nor shoal, nor rock

Could lie that way I knew.

　　　　　　　　The strange red star

Came swimming from that low horizon far,

Over the level of the watery plain,

Paving a ghastly pathway o'er the main,

And all the breadth of sea grew pale between

Where myriad fish in thronging shoals were seen

Gliding in terror from the hateful sight,

While, underneath, the dim depths glittered bright

With eyes of fierce sea-creatures, quelled in awe,

Grim sharks agape to glut their greedy maw ;

And soon I spied the direful deck where sate,

Like councillors on high, exempt, elate,

The fiends triumphant in their fiery state !

How should I pray : ' God guard us '?   Draw not nigh !

There is no death reserved for me to die

Beyond the death I ventured then.   Our ship

Lay as becalmed.   Striving for voice, my lip

Hung speechless, for I marked the ghastly crew

So pale—and all their bark one flame !   I knew

Their prow was bound for Venice, yet I strove

To frame such question as response might move

From damnéd spirits—and still I could not speak,

And lip and arm fell motionless and weak.

The devils read my thought, and one alone

(For our ship crossed their bow), in chiding tone,

Cried : 'Friend, give place!   Our way across the sea

Lies where thy bark rides idly.   Know that we

May turn not to the left nor right.   No helm

Is ours, and when the surging billows whelm

Less crafts, we sweep triumphant o'er the main,

Unswerving.   Lo! our profit is thy gain,

Whose summons drew us to the ungodly town,

From pinnacle to rotting pile our own!'

At first I stared, I could not understand

That it was I had brought this burning brand

Towards our city.   Then I looked to land,

And understood.   Was it not very plain?

I thought my soul's thirst quenched—but then again

I murmured : 'I love Venice.'—No more weak

Hung lip or arm, the blood flushed in my cheek,

I cried : 'For Venice' sake,' and raised mine arm

To form, from cross-wise yard and mast, the charm

From which, I knew, the foe must flee.   The sail

Hung idly flapping in the gathering gale.

I heard the fiends' shrill cry : 'For Venice' good !

Rival thine ancient foe in gratitude,

Then come and make thy home with us in Hell !'

I knew it must be so.   I knew the spell

Of Satan on my soul.   I felt the power

Granted by God to serve Him one last hour,

Then fall for ever as the curse had wrought.

I climbed aloft.   My brain had grown one thought,

One hope, one purpose.   And I heard the hiss

Of raging disappointment, loth to miss

Its prey—I heard the lapping of the flame,

That through the blenchéd figures went and came,

Darting in frenzy to the devils' yell.

I set that cross on high, and cried : 'To Hell

My soul for ever, and my deed to God !

Once Venice guarded safe, let this vile clod

Drift where fate will !'

And then (the hideous laugh

Of fiends in full possession, keen to quaff

The wine of one new soul not weak with tears,

Pealing like ruinous thunder in mine ears)

I fell, and heard no more.   The pale day broke

Through lazar-windows, when once more I woke,

Remembering I might no more dare to pray.

Sir, you have helped me—in a different way,

Not as the priest might help—for the priest stands

'Twixt God and man with deprecating hands

For mercy—but my doom is sealed above.

O endless justice with the heart of love !

Past supplication, still I raise my hymn

Of praise, because, beyond the starlight dim,

He dwells and understands.   All creatures praise

His name, and shall not, in His mighty ways,

Hell's host prove God's creation ?   Angels, men,—

Aye, men and devils—for beyond His ken

Can nothing live, nor be but by His will,

And I in Hell shall live God's creature still.

Why do you linger?   He will send anon.

I thought, just now, the dreaded face was gone

That vexed my soul with still reproving eyes.

Good friend, you will forget in Paradise."

I know not if I spoke.   Perhaps he felt

The silent awe.   I lingered where I knelt.

But while I sought for words, the spirit was flown,

Uncomforted, on the dark night, alone.

    Turning to leave, I found my grave old friend

Gazing beside me on the wondrous end,

And soon he spoke : "Just entering on the strife

You gaze, as I, laden with spoils of life,

Gaze hopeless on the problem aye unsolved,

Each knowing all his aims therein involved.

What if this deed—no deed—prove nobler far

Than theirs who sit to judge of peace or war,

With whom in truth rests Venice' fate to-night,

While this man gave his own soul's morning light

(Or so he deemed) for that same Venice' sake?

Who knows how soon the dawning light may break

Over our city abandoned and betrayed

By hearts that withered in her glory's shade,

While this man traced her splendour's flawless wheel

Lacking life's axle?   Where is false or real?

Rather say : ' Here is lost in timeless night

One useless ray the more of morning light.' "

Homeward I paced along the starlight quay,

Heard the far cannon booming o'er the sea,

And learned the council must disperse anon

With resolutions weak—while on and on,

Pressed from without the wolvish foe for prey,

And deep within muttered the throng at bay.

OPHELION

DRAMATIS PERSONÆ

Night   *Death*   *Dawn*

OPHELION, *a Scholar*

Night

O'ER the crocus-sprinkled meadows

When the sun was sinking low,

And eve, like a gray mist rising

Led forth a star in heaven,

Mother and child stood gazing

On the glitter far below;

Far beyond the long dark shadows

    Sloping eastward from the brow

        Of the purple hills to westward ;

        Far beyond the rich low champaign,

        Gazing on the crystal glitter

Where the blue waves ebb and flow.

And the mother sang a song

    That was made in years of old,

When men were fair as gods,

        And the gods were seen of men,

    When the singer's heart was glad and bold,

    The days that come never again.

" Phœbus, Lord of the light of heaven,

Lord of the light of the rising morn,

Strong in the lightning speed of thine arrow,

Bright with the splendour of days unborn,

Hail, strong conqueror !   Hail, all-victorious !

Low at thy feet lies the serpent of night.

Phœbus, thy brow, than the noontide more glorious,

Bend on thy suppliants, Light of light !

" Lady of heaven most pure and holy,

Artemis, fleet as the flying deer,

Glide through the dusk like a silver shadow,

Mirror thy brow in the lonely mere.

We with the break of day will follow

The light-hooved roe through woodland and hollow,

But with garlands and songs of the maidens bright,

May we first win thy favour, Lady of light."

Now the wind breathed laden with chill of dew,

Creeping over the furrowy grass,

The trembling grass of the upland meadow,

While far in the lingering light of even,

The hills lay circled with gleaming blue,

Bathed in the molten gold of heaven,

Folded at rest in purple shadow.

And in dusky gloom of ferny dell

The low wind's murmurs rose and fell,

And the bee had fled from the dewy clover,

And forth on the night came the beetle, the rover,

Winging his way through the dusky gloom,

And striking his wings, with sudden boom,

'Gainst the hollow oak by the deep-delved well.

And mother and child wended their way

Up the low steps of the winding road,

D

Through the olive grove in the mild Spring weather,

    And the child pressed close by his mother's side

For fear of dread shapes in their dim abode,

In the twisted olives gnarled and gray

    (Where the pallid wind-flower, scarce descried

In the shifting shade, droops weary-eyed

    And the moth a violet's breath divines),

    Till at last they stood 'neath the tall dark pines,

And passed through the sweet white heather,

Where the risen moon in the pale blue sky

Silvered the pines.   The Eastern sea,

    With a crystal ripple of liquid waters,

Smiled on her advent, and far and nigh

    The frore light rested on river and lea.

"Mother, thy song was of Phœbus and Artemis.

    Phœbus and Artemis, where are they?

Where is great Pan that rules o'er the woodlands?

When is the dance of the nymphs and satyrs?

Are all these fled from our land away?"

But the mother plucked at the sweet white heather.

" Peace, thou prattler! the gods are here.

But Phœbus sits in the sunny heaven,

And when the moon shines over hill and hollow,

Then Artemis chaseth the flying deer.

And great Pan's altar thou knowest well,

By the brook where the minnows glide and dart;

Thou knowest the wreaths, thou knowest the smell

Of the incense breathing blue coils of vapour,

What time the woodland echoes follow

The murmurous prayer—where thy grandsire stood,

When the mildew blighted the vine on the lea,

And slew a kid for the hapless hart

The huntsmen smote in the sacred pale.

But the nymphs and satyrs dance in the wood

When thou art at play.   It is not for thee

   To question the gods, or to lift the veil

      That hides the immortals from wiser than thou,

From thy grandsire, and from me."

Now mother and child stand by the hut,

  While the moon grows bright in the deepening sky,

   The low turf hut by the bubbling spring,

Where the flocks in their wattled pens are shut ;

      And the fierce gaunt watch-dog fawns at their feet,

      And the hoary grandsire comes forth to meet

   Mother and child (yet lingering

  Where the dewless path spreads, broad and dry)

As they bring from the town, where strange merchants

     throng

By the bright sea, tools for their household meet,

A painted jar and a crowbar strong,

  And a pot of incense sweet.

Ophelion

Ah, strange and powerful !

Ah, sweet and wonderful !

As if a spell were broken, as if the years were new.

Came that music from my heart ?

Do I hear the young years singing ?

Will they loose me from the toils the ages round me threw ?

Fade not, sweet voice, into the weary night !

Restore that hope which I had dreamt immortal,

That hope which shivered at the blast of death !

Shine on me through the shadows, radiant angel of light !

Loose the fetters of my soul by the power of thy

breath,

As the earth's deep bonds are loosened,

As the buds are freed in Spring.

Yet wait !   The whole comes back to me again,

　　Image on image.   Lo, my mother there,

Ankle-deep in the moss—after the rain

　　It grows so soft—and all that weight of hair

Scarce lifted by the wind !   She stands there calling

　　The goats down from the rock, for the sheep are in

　　　　the fold,

And Argos lamed with a thorn, and the dew is falling,

　　And some one saw a wolf prowling last night on the

　　　　wold.

Then a journey—what was that ?   They were talking of

　　a journey.

　　We came down from the heather, through the olives

　　　　to the plain,

When the path was wet with dew, and the birds were

　　singing early,

And the pale sun shot long gleams athwart the whiten-

 ing grain.

All the long day we walked, till the sun rode high in

 heaven,

 The clay by the pools was cracked, the dust lay white

 in the road;

At eve we stood on a hill and saw at our feet a city

 Where the beams of the setting sun on wall and garden

 glowed.

Ah, Night, thy tale is mine—yet scarce so fair

As I had dreamed but now.   In that white town

Dwelt the old master, wise in words and rules—

The commentator's restless brain—the soul

That, seeking, misses still the ways of light,

Groping between the parchments.   But his wife

Plucked me sweet purple grapes, and said: "Dear child,

Come live with us among the vines.   Methinks

They thrive but poorly on your windy hill."

Then was I glad, and answered : "Aye, with mother,

And we will bring great Argos from the hill,

Chloë and old Timæus and the rest,

For you have grapes enough for all of us."

But silent came my mother from the house,

And they two wept—while I ran to the court

And watched the slave fitting a scarlet bridle

On a white mule. "Thy mother goes," he spake,

And hung the jingling bridle on the wall.

Eleven years I dwelt among the vines ;

Eleven years the master's word was law ;

Eleven years I laboured in the gloom.

Then the change came. The long slow task was done,

The scholar grown beyond the master's strength—

Sad master, toiling down the trodden path—

Who sorrowfully bade me soar and sink,

Blessed me and sent me forth alone to Athens.

Sadly at first I pondered on the past,

And sadly rose to meet the coming years,

But, when I saw the black ship cut the foam,

I felt a wondrous joy to see strange lands,

And, sailing onward, questioned them that knew

Of each low headland, islet, creek, or strait,

Till, the third night, one told me: " With the dawn

Thou shalt see Athens." While the stars crept out

Upon the deck I sat, in the cool gloom,

And listened to the plashing of the waves

About the poop and the low creaking yards,

And watched the soft mild outlines, blue on blue,

Of the steep hills and headlands—star on star

Glanced in the heaving waters, changing still,

Until the first white streak dimmed in the east

The golden starlight—then came one and said :

" Look, Sunium, yonder, and the silver mines !"

But what I looked upon with straining eyes

Filled all my soul.   I could but gaze and gaze,

Aegina rising as the sky grew redder,

Salamis, Athens in a maze of light !

Here, then, I dwelt, for this was truly Athens,

But not the Athens I had framed in dreams

On summer noons, beneath the glistening vines.

This seems so far—as if a time of change

Had broken through my life—as if I lost

A world, yet found a world—so lost and found,

And lost and sought again, until each world

Became a matter of less moment to me,

And my own life and ways grew all in all.

And sometimes, when I sat to watch the stars

Over Mount Parnes in the sad dark heaven,

There grew a murmur in me : Fair ?   Why fair ?

Why fair, those little sparks of wandering light ?

Why fair the weight of waters or yon breadth

Of rolling land? Oh, but each breaking day,

With all the light and gladness of its East,

And all the trembling pallor of its West,

With all its surging sea of fire and gold,

And pale blue reaches of untroubled sky,

What is it but the sad recurring call

To life and labour and to pain and death?

Children and fools, we call it sweet to live,

And sweet to gaze upon the eternal heaven.

What profit we by its eternal strength,

Save as a rod to mete our weakness by,

And count its rolling courses for the limit

Of our own lives? O weary, weary world!

O gift of life! slowly to count the stars,

Then say: So many millions move for ever,

And I must die that told their myriad spheres!

Nay, there were other thoughts. My heart beat high

With some wild hope that Hellas might arise—

Another Hellas in the light of Rome—

Calling its glory from the past, and shedding

New light upon new life—as if the dead

That sleep in nameless tombs could rise once more,

And gaze, with that old glory round their brows,

Upon the world of men I lived amongst,

And not cry: "Let us seek our graves again!"

Ah! but one Autumn evening, chill and drear,

I sat alone beside the flickering wick

And pored on some dull blinding chart till, weary,

I raised my head and looked without.   A gust

Blew clear between the swaying cypress tips,

And showed the full red breadth of evening sky,

And thin moon waning to her shivering rest.

Then the wind ceased, and all the cypress spires

Sprang close and dark, and hid the louring sky,

Leaving the empty death-like silence round me

Where I stood dazzled by the flickering wick

Till it flared up and died and the last gleam

Grew ashen pale, then vanished in the gloom

That deepened cold and lonely.   I went forth

Under the plane-trees by the windy wall,

And watched the Eastern starlight cold and clear,

And while I gazed I thought of Rome and Hellas—

Of all that was and all that might have been

And now could never be—for night is long,

And death is swift, and every tomb fast sealed.

Night

Sealed !

Aye, fast sealed,

For ever, in the night

Of the doom that never was repealed.

Then turn thy thoughts away,

Where the level morning light

Shall gleam athwart the sea

That knoweth no decay;

 For it ebbeth aye, and floweth,

 And waneth where it groweth,

 Like corn the reaper soweth,

Or reapeth on the lea;

Where the land of Southern day

Seemed once so fair to thee;

Where from wreathéd myrtle bowers,

Through the tangled maze of flowers,

 Low sweet voices laugh and call,

By gleaming marble towers,

 Columned court and carven hall

(Aye new roses bud 'neath showers

 Of the red rose-leaves that fall);

Where the golden Southern sunlight

 Lieth soft on land and sea,

'Neath the gleam of dancing blossoms,

Dreaming on things to be,

Dream on, and on for ever,

Till all the world to thee

Seem as, between the palm-leaves,

A glimpse of rippling sea.

Ophelion

So sweet—so wondrous sweet—and not for ever.

To dream and dream! Aye, but each dream? What

then?

Oh, I have tried it. Is there nothing more?

Nothing yet left to make it sweet to breathe

Beneath the harmless heaven? No force, no power

To mould the world about our dream and prove

The subtle shadow's feature in the light

Of noonday sun? Oh, this might once have been—

But I am weary—weary with the weight

Of life, and sense of being—all too weary

To hope or strive as once I strove and hoped.

Death

Listen to me, that call thee from the shadow

    Of day insufferably bright !

Listen ! thy lot was never cast with morning,

    Thy life hath no more part in light.

Let the dawn sing and let the first light quiver !

Thy life keeps flowing, flowing, like a river,

That through a dusky cave doth bend and shiver

    Down to the cold still pool of night.

Ophelion

Aye, Death, I listen.   Sing me, thou, my doom,

For thou art master now !   Why not ere now ?

Why should warm life have twined so sweet and close

About my soul before its growth was cut ?

Once there were blossoms, nests of summer birds.

It brought no fruit, ye say? Take it for thine,

That once seemed mine. I could not strive again

Now all things seem so sweet. I could but seek

The old worn pathway up the sandy hill,

And sing the old sweet song as night grows blue.

Death

All that was once to be,

All that is lost to thee,

All that shall never be,

    Weigh it, and pause, and cry :

"This shall return no more.

Summer shall paint the floor

Of earth with flowers o'er ;

    This shall not come to me."

Hold it and grasp, and try

(While year by year slips by)

E

To bind the wings that fly,

 Or hold within thy door

The fluttering heart of Time ;

For Earth is past her prime,

And thou art bound to climb,

 And seek for evermore.

See the light surging low !

See how the first streaks glow !

So did thy gladness grow,

 So shall it fade and fall ;

Fade with the morning's prime,

Fade with the Autumn's rime.

Loose thy weak hold on time !

 Death is enough for thee.

Weary thy grasp, and weak !

So much is left to seek !

So much is left to speak !

 And night enfoldeth all.

Lay thee down soft to rest

With the world hushed in thy breast,

And thy grave the wild bird's nest,

For all that is to be !

Ophelion

Ay, gentle Death, thy words methinks sound sweetest,

And calm thy promise, as if all fulfilled.

I could die now.

Clear dayspring ! Now—for ever ?

And lose thy light of dawn beyond the night ?

O blameless majesty of earth and sky !

Methinks that on thy brow is writ the morning,

And round thy feet the stars sing to the dawn.

And while I pass away they sing for ever,

Singing and singing to the dawn to come

When I am dust and ashes. Let one word

Break from thy silent lips of rolling gold,

Burst in upon the night, and death and darkness,

Roll the dim shadows back and flood with light,

With sweet last light, the ashes of this spirit

Half in the gloom—hear me that cry to thee!

O light, if death must come—let death be light!

Dawn

Arise, greet thou the glory

That brimmeth o'er the heavens!

Thy life and death are shadows,

    When I pass thou shalt not see.

Yet arise, cry to the morning!

Raise thine eyes to heaven's new splendour!

The light hath laid the darkness,

    And the noontide is to be!

For this day a soul shall perish,

Yet the morrow's dawn shall cherish

Another soul in gladness

   To gaze on sky and sea.

I am no voice of twilight;

I am the voice of dawning;

Thou that longest for the daybreak,

   Lift thine eyes and cry to me!

Then ring out, ye sons of morning,

Your song of joy and warning,

For the rending of the shadow,

   For the light on land and sea!

For hope lies in the morrow,

That brings new joy and sorrow

To the souls that wait and wonder,

   And the souls that are to be.

A FRIAR'S STORY

(See the " Fioretti di San Francesco ")

FRATE MASSEO, Angelo and I

    Were witness to the tale recorded here.

It was scarce evening yet, and in the sky

    The thin white crescent moon did but appear,

    While through the Summer evening, from the mere

That lies towards Ancona, by the sea,

    We heard the frogs' sharp trill, and sweet and clear

Sang the cicala from the blasted tree,

'Neath which, folk say, a cursèd idol used to be.

There was one Eastern window, strait and high.

    Masseo stood beneath, and watched where lay

On his low pallet, as the weeks rolled by,

    Frate Giovanni (so he bade us say,

    Else had we called him Padre). Day by day

We gathered round him when the evening fell,

    After the vesper-hymn, and he would pray

And talk with us a little. He would tell

Of God's great mercy—this his life could teach as well.

Only, that evening, when we turned to go,

    He raised his head and called us : "Will ye stay

And watch one hour with me, my children? Lo,

    I shall not tarry longer. I would say

    Some few short words before I pass away."

Frate Masseo, Angelo and I

    Knelt on the ground beside him—I to pray,

Masseo wept, but Angelo drew nigh

And kissed his hand—to him it seemed less hard to die.

Then we bent near and listened, for the words

    Of him who stands by Death fall few and low,

And ever and anon night-screeching birds

    Would drown his voice with clamour.   Angelo

    Held fast his hand.   He spoke: "My friends, you know

My term is wellnigh reached—threescore and ten—

    And no more way is left for me to go.

This night I pass from out the world of men,

And on Death's scroll my name is writ with brazen pen.

"I lie and muse of many a vanished day,

    But most of one near Penna on the hill,

Where from my father's house we looked away

    Over Spoleto to the sea.   A rill,

    Fed with the snows each springtide, turned his mill,

And you could hear the busy clacking wheel

    Through the long summer evenings—else as still

As were mid-winter here—yet now they reel

And fade before mine eyes, as when we used to kneel

" In the dark chapel on the mountain brow,

   And then come forth and gaze upon the plain

That stretched before us to the sea—as now

   You see Ancona and the mere. The grain

   Golden around Spoleto, the blue main

And the red sails from Venice—all were blent

   Before our dazzled eyes, like the bright vane

That whirls whene'er the Northern blast is sent,

And we stood gazing still, for very wonderment.

" But all this world seems little to me now

   That I have come so near my day of rest.

Only God leave me breath to tell you how

   At first He called me to Himself, and blest

   For ever be His name, for on His breast

The peace awaits me which can never fade.

   Ah, friend, His word is light ! When in the West

This night's sweet moon hath sunk, I shall have laid

My soul in His strong hands that hath so long delayed.

" I was a child—a boy, like Angelo,

    And knew not yet God's will.   I could but pray,

But not in peace, my children, for to know

    His will alone gives peace.   I sought a way

    To win that Paradise, that perfect day,

That garden blooming round the throne of gold,

    Whence blessèd Dorothy, as all men say,

Sent fragrant flowers and fruit in days of old,

Christ's holy martyr—this my mother often told.

" And now came rumours through the country-side

    Of blessèd Francis and his heavenly light,

And how he was to God's own poor a guide

    And helper of all such as in the night

    Did stray and wander, bringing gift of sight

Free to the blind, and how he walked in faith,

    Keeping his taper ever burning bright

To light men's steps through the dim halls of death,

And holding, as of small account, this mortal breath.

" A night in April, soft and calm as now,

    I lay and wondered how to find that way

That leads to God's fair garden. One white bough

    Of budding almond-blossoms bent its spray

    Athwart the casement. Glad at heart I lay

And watched the threaded stars that seemed to lie

    Among the twigs, when lo, a sudden ray

(Draw closer, children) lit the room and I

Gazed breathless, for I straightway knew that God was nigh.

" And then there came two angels—for the light

    That floods the morning sea was on their brow,

And all their wings with gold and azure dight.

    Each bare a flaming sword. I strove to bow

    My head before their splendour. Weak enow

These words of mine, as weak as then my will,

    For I could only gaze on them, and now,

After long years, I have not gazed my fill.

Nigh threescore years have I, Lord, waited on Thy will.

" One summoned me and said : ' Giovanni, go

 To-morrow to San Stefano and pray

And hear God's servant, Fra Gentile. Know

 It is his will to guide thee to that day

 Which passeth the world's glory. Long the way

Thou first must journey.' Then I turned and sought,

 And saw their face no more. The breaking day

Had filled the chamber. Oh, the change it brought !

The way to work God's will ! I had no other thought.

" And forth I wandered on my way. I took

 Nor staff nor scrip, for this was Christ's behest.

But ere the goal the force wellnigh forsook

 My childish limbs. I lay me down to rest

 In the cold church, and murmuring : ' So is best,

For so my journey surely is at end.

 Lord, show me Thy bright heaven, Thy name be blest !'

I waited. It was not His will to send

His angel for me yet. I could but bide and bend.

" I tarried till the doors thronged with the crowd,

    God's people who, from all the land around,

Flocked thither for His word.   Now clear and loud

    Preached Fra Gentile.—Had I not, then, found

    That road to heaven, that path beyond life's bound.?

Or must I start upon my way again ?

    I lay there motionless as in a swound.

I could not stir beneath such load of pain,

But listened sadly with a heart full little fain.

" When all his words were ended, loth I turned

    To leave the church.   Near the slow-swinging door

A friar begged for alms, and something burned

    Within my heart.   'God's peace be with thee ! more

    I cannot give.'   The night was chill and hoar.

Through the dark portal shone the frosty moon.

    I waited, wondering.   'Is all hope, then, o'er ?

I thought to find Thy garden, Lord, so soon,

And here is night on earth.   Oh, lead me to Thy noon !'

" It was an aged friar, thin and pale,

   And shrinking in his cassock from the cold.

The freezing moonlight, like a strange thin veil,

   Softened his brow. Without, the churchyard mould

   Cracked 'neath the last quick steps. Half in a fold

Of his loose serge, half on the cold hard stone

   I lay me down. Somewhile the old man told

His patient beads. I gave a little moan—

He paused and marvelled how the wind did sigh and groan.

" But I took heart and cried : 'Good father, say

   Where he is gone that preached God's word but now,

Frate Gentile. Do not say me nay,

   For I must speak with him.' The old man's brow,

   Wrinkled in thought. 'I'll show thee soon enow.'

He led me where the friars dwell—beside

   The lazar-house. Right warm and fair, I trow,

Seemed the small blaze, whereby he bade me bide

Among the holy friars, by the broad chimney-side,

" 'Till Fra Gentile came.   Then I arose

    And told, all solemn, how I sought the way

To God's own Paradise, where ever grows

    The tree of life, where cometh no decay

    Sullying the face of that eternal day ;

And then I cried : 'Oh, if it be thy will,

    Good father, force me to no long delay !

Let me strip off the world for Christ !'—and still

I bless God's name for this, on His own heaven's bright sill.

" So I became a friar, poor in God,

    Rich in the loss of this world's little strife,

Blessèd in all I leave—the graveyard sod

    Mouldering with death—the fragments of a life.

    And when I think how this world's day is rife

With pain and darkness, then I bless God's name,

    The one clear gleam in midmost night—a knife

To cut this tangled knot of woes—the frame

On which the stars are hung—the ceaseless burning flame.

" And I have wandered—North to Aquitaine,

    And Southward far as Capua. And men say,

' A poor old friar.' Oh, for cold or pain,

    Or death, how should I care, who hoped alway

    In heaven's own dawn at end of each long day ?

But now it is the blessèd end of all—

    Each path I trod, each weary hill that lay

Before my feet. Now leave me not to fall.

Lo, yonder, Lord, Thy towers—Thy city's golden wall !"

.

He lay there dead. Now I am old and gray.

    Masseo sleeps beside him where both lie

In Penna. Angelo has left God's way.

    That night we knelt beneath the silent sky,

    Frate Masseo, Angelo and I,

And prayed for all poor souls in sorrow dwelling,

    And prayed to live in Christ, in Christ to die,

Like that meek spirit for whom night was knelling

The farewell song of earth, up the low hill-slope swelling.

BEATRICE PORTINARI

As I was gazing on the purple ring,

Where round the hills dark clouds hung far and nigh,

Methought I saw one star-white opening,

Where angels circled in the silent sky.

I raised mine eyes again—dreaming that thou

Shouldst mount with light step to that angel choir ;

They passed away, and then I saw thy brow

Changed and transfigured in the sunset fire.

F

VENETIAN SONG

Leaning between carved stone and stone,
As glossy birds peer from a nest
Scooped in the crumbling trunk where rest
Their freckled eggs, I pause alone
And linger in the light awhile,
Waiting for joy to come to me—
Only the dawn beyond yon isle,
Only the sunlight on the sea.

I gaze—then turn and ply my loom,

    Or broider blossoms close beside ;

    The morning world lies warm and wide,

But here is dim, cool silent gloom,

      Gold crust and crimson velvet pile,

        And not one face to smile on me—

      Only the dawn beyond yon isle,

        Only the sunlight on the sea.

Over the world the splendours break

    Of morning light and noontide glow,

    And when the broad red sun sinks low,

And in the wave long shadows shake,

      Youths, maidens, glad with song and wile,

        Glide and are gone, and leave with me

      Only the dawn beyond yon isle,

        Only the sunlight on the sea.

MORTALITY

O WESTERN wold, that softly sleepest,
And thou, wan East, that waking weepest
　　Because thy day is done—
　　What though his course be run?
　Over yon hill-tops, faint and far,
　Shall glimmer evening and morning star,
Till the watch of night that darkens deepest
　　Lead back thy sun.

O wintry tree, the wild winds, wailing,

Are every barren bough unveiling,

　　Because warm days are o'er.

　　Why creak with branches hoar?

　Each dun dry leaf of frost's undoing

　Leaves the firm bud for Spring's young wooing,

For rise of sap and blossoms prevailing—

　　No Winter more.

But thou, sad World, so restless pining

In blight of Winter past divining,

　　Because thy joy is flown,

　　And thou art left alone ;

　Ever thy sunset fire must shimmer,

　And aye thy woodland gold must glimmer,

Spring may not meet thee, nor morning, inclining

　　Down from God's throne.

HYMN TO PERSEPHONE

Oh, fill my cup, Persephone,

   With dim red wine of Spring,

      And drop therein a faded leaf

      Plucked from the Autumn's bearded sheaf,

Whence, dread one, I may quaff to thee,

   While all the woodlands ring.

Oh, fill my heart, Persephone,

    With thine immortal pain,

        That lingers round the willow bowers

        In memories of old happy hours,

When thou didst wander fair and free

    O'er Enna's blooming plain.

Oh, fill my soul, Persephone,

    With music all thine own !

        Teach me some song thy childhood knew,

        Lisped in the meadow's morning dew,

Or chant, on this high windy lea,

    Thy godhead's ceaseless moan.

HYMN TO APOLLO

APOLLO, lord of lyre and song,

    Shall the world win me to forget

The sweet still hours I've roamed among

    The meads thou lovest yet?

Those morning meadows, wet with dew,

    Whereon thy sun lay warm and wide,

Where slender white-weed blossoms grew

    The waving grass beside?

Shall I forget long days in Spring

 When, led by thy sweet influence,

I sought, where shallow waters sing,

 Thy song surpassing sense?

Shall I forget thy hand was laid

 Upon my brow with morning's sun?

Or how I wandered in thy shade,

 And watched the river run,

Beneath the crimson-tufted larch,

 By fronds of fern that soft unroll,

What time the windy gusts of March

 Made music in my soul?